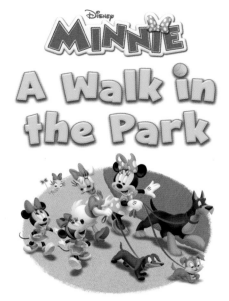

Minnie
A Walk in the Park

Based on the episode written by Jennifer Heftler
Adapted by Gina Gold
Illustrated by Loter, Inc.

ABDOBOOKS.COM

Reinforced library bound edition published in 2019 by Spotlight, a division of ABDO, PO Box 398166, Minneapolis, Minnesota 55439. Spotlight produces high-quality reinforced library bound editions for schools and libraries. Published by agreement with Disney Press, an imprint of Disney Book Group.

Printed in the United States of America, North Mankato, Minnesota.
092018   012019

Disney PRESS
New York • Los Angeles

THIS BOOK CONTAINS
RECYCLED MATERIALS

Library of Congress Control Number: 2017960982

Publisher's Cataloging-in-Publication Data

Names: Gold, Gina, author. | Heftler, Jennifer, author. | Loter, Inc., illustrator.
Title: Minnie: A walk in the park / by Gina Gold and Jennifer Heftler; illustrated by Loter, Inc.
Description: Minneapolis, MN : Spotlight, 2019 | Series: World of reading level pre-1
Summary: Minnie, Daisy, and Cuckoo-Loca take their pups for a quiet walk at the park, until the pups see and smell a hot dog cart. Can Minnie get this dog walk under control?
Identifiers: ISBN 9781532141836 (lib. bdg.)
Subjects: LCSH: Mickey Mouse Clubhouse (Television program)--Juvenile fiction. | Mouse, Minnie (Fictitious character)--Juvenile fiction. | Dog walking--Juvenile fiction. | Readers (Primary)--Juvenile fiction.
Classification: DDC [E]--dc23

Spotlight
A Division of ABDO
abdobooks.com

Everyone is making bows.
The dogs get in the way.

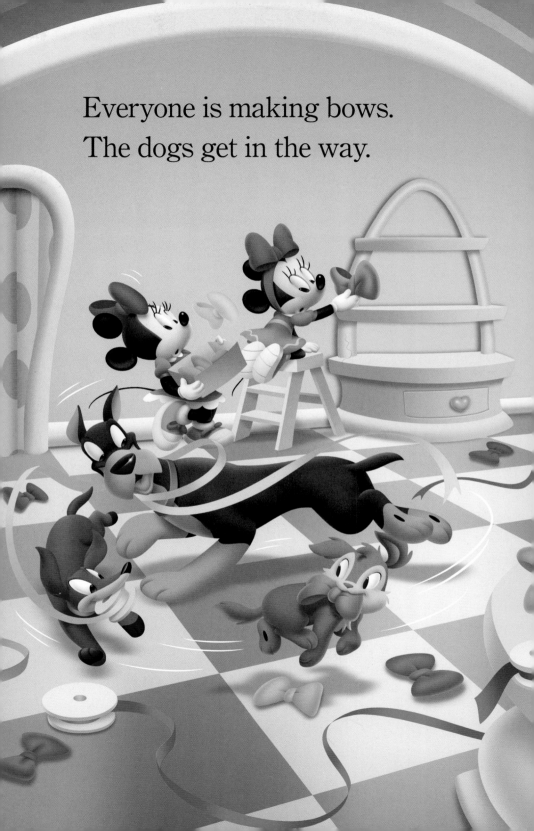

"We cannot work," Daisy says.
"How about a walk?" says Minnie.

"Dogs love to walk," says Minnie.
"Me too," Millie says.

"Look!" says Cuckoo-Loca.
"Hot dogs!"

"I want one," says Daisy.

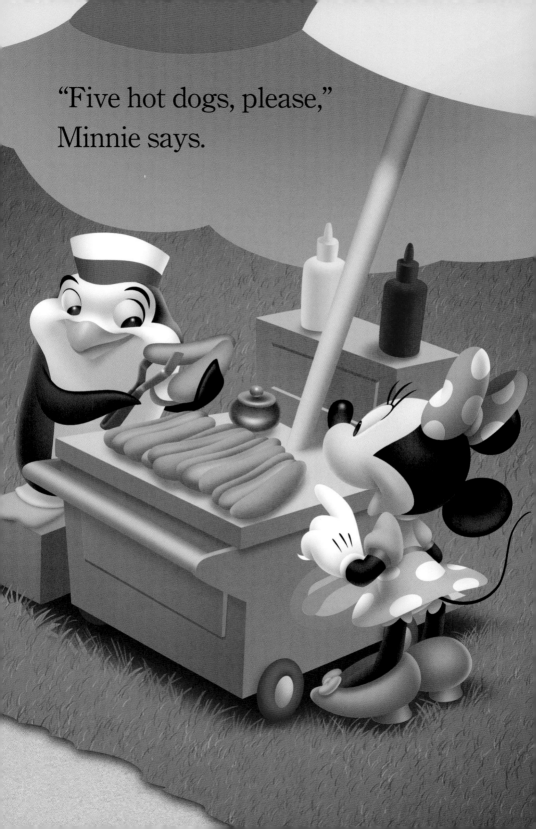

"Five hot dogs, please," Minnie says.

The hot dogs smell yummy.

Ella grabs a hot dog. She runs.
"Come back!" says the hot dog man.

"Stop!" the twins cry.

"Dogs on the run!" says Cuckoo-Loca.

"Help me!" says Minnie.

"The dogs run fast!" Minnie says.

"They are over there!"
says Cuckoo-Loca.

Ella jumps.
The ball machine turns on.

The balls bounce.
"Look out!" says Cuckoo-Loca.

Minnie shuts off the machine.
"Time to clean up," she says.

Wait! Ella sees something.
What does Ella see?
She sees a squirrel.

Ella chases the squirrel.
"Slow down!" says Daisy.

The dogs pull Daisy.
"Help!" she says.

"Come on!" says Minnie.
"Daisy needs us."

The dogs keep running.

Daisy cannot stop them.

Daisy goes up.

Daisy swings.

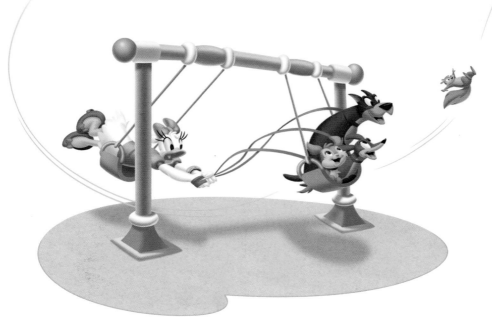

Daisy slides down.

Daisy goes around and flies off.

Daisy lands in the sand.
"Are you okay?" says Minnie.

"We cannot chase the dogs,"
Daisy says.
"It is too hot," says Cuckoo-Loca.

"Hot . . ." says Minnie. "Dogs . . .
That's it!"

Minnie has a plan.

"Ready, set, go!" says Minnie.
Hot dogs fly.

The dogs stop to catch them.

"Now," says Minnie.
"We can walk."

Wait! Ella sees something.
What does Ella see?
She sees a cat!

The cat runs. Ella runs.
The dogs run.

"Not again," says Minnie. "Run!"